A LITTLE PILGRIM
IN THE UNSEEN

A LITTLE PILGRIM IN THE UNSEEN

MRS. OLIPHANT

WILDSIDE PRESS

A LITTLE PILGRIM IN THE UNSEEN

This edition published 2005 by Wildside Press, LLC.
www.wildsidepress.com

In Memoriam
E.C.
25TH FEBRUARY 1882

The sympathetic reader will easily understand that the following pages were never meant to be connected with any author's name. They sprang out of those thoughts that arise in the heart, when the door of the Unseen has been suddenly opened close by us; and are little more than a wistful attempt to follow a gentle soul which never knew doubt into the New World, and to catch a glimpse of something of its glory through her simple and child-like eyes.

CONTENTS

A LITTLE PILGRIM
IN THE UNSEEN

She had been talking of dying only the evening before, with a friend, and had described her own sensations after a long illness when she had been at the point of death. "I suppose," she said, "that I was as nearly gone as any one ever was to come back again. There was no pain in it, only a sense of sinking down, down—through the bed as if nothing could hold me or give me support enough—but no pain." And then they had spoken of another friend in the same circumstances, who also had come back from the very verge, and who described her sensations as those of one floating upon a summer sea without pain or suffering, in a lovely nook of the Mediterranean, blue as the sky. These soft and soothing images of the passage which all men dread had been talked over with low voices, yet with smiles and a grateful sense that "the warm precincts of the cheerful day" were once more familiar to both. And very cheerfully she went to rest that night, talking of what was to be done on the morrow, and fell asleep sweetly in her little room, with its shaded light and curtained window, and little pictures on the dim walls. All was quiet in the house: soft breathing of the sleepers, soft murmuring of the spring wind outside, a wintry moon very clear and full in the skies, a little town all hushed and quiet, everything lying defenceless, unconscious, in the safe keeping of God.

How soon she woke no one can tell. She woke and lay quite still, half roused, half hushed, in that soft languor that attends a happy waking. She was happy always in the peace of a heart that was humble and faithful and pure, but yet had been used to wake to a consciousness of little pains and troubles, such as even to her meekness were sometimes hard to bear. But on this morning there were none of these. She lay in a kind of hush of happiness and ease, not caring to make any further movement, lingering over the sweet sensation of that waking. She had no desire to move nor to break the spell of the silence and peace. It was still very early, she supposed, and probably it might be hours yet before any one came to call her. It might even be that she should sleep again. She had no wish to move, she lay in such luxurious ease and calm. But by and by, as she came to full possession of her waking senses, it appeared to her that there was some change in the atmosphere, in the scene. There began to steal into the air about her the soft dawn as of a summer morning, the lovely blueness of the first opening of daylight before the sun. It could not be the light of the moon which she had seen before she went to bed; and all was so still that it could not be the bustling wintry day which comes at that time of the year late, to find the world awake before it. This was different; it was like the summer dawn, a soft suffusion of light growing every moment. And by and by it occurred to her that she was not in the little room where she had lain down. There were no dim walls or roof, her little pictures were all gone, the curtains at her window. The discovery gave her no uneasiness in that delightful calm. She lay still to think of it all, to wonder, yet undisturbed. It half amused her that these things should be changed, but did not rouse her yet with any shock of alteration. The light grew fuller and fuller round, growing into day, clearing her eyes from the sweet mist of the first waking. Then she raised herself upon her arm. She was not in her room, she was in no scene she knew. Indeed it was scarcely a scene at all—nothing but light, so soft and lovely that it soothed and caressed her eyes. She thought all at once of a summer morning when she was a child, when she had woke in the deep night which yet was day, early—so early that the birds were scarcely astir—and had risen up with a delicious sense of daring, and of being all alone in the mystery of the sunrise, in the unawakened world which lay at her feet to be explored, as if she were Eve just entering upon Eden. It was curious how all those childish sensations, long forgotten, came back to her as she found herself so unexpectedly out of her sleep in the open air and light. In the recollection of that lovely hour, with a smile at herself, so different as she now knew herself to be, she was moved to rise and look a little more closely about her and see where she was.

When I call her a little Pilgrim, I do not mean that she was a child; on the contrary, she was not even young. She was little by nature, with as little flesh and blood as was consistent with mortal life; and she was one of those who are always little for love. The tongue found diminutives for her; the heart kept her in a perpetual youth. She was so modest and so gentle that she always came last so long as there was any one whom she could put before her. But this little body, and the soul which was not little, and the heart which was big and great, had known all the round of sorrows that fill a woman's life, without knowing any of its warmer blessings. She had nursed the sick, she had entertained the weary, she had consoled the dying. She had gone about the world, which had no prize nor recompense for her, with a smile. Her little presence had been always bright. She was not clever; you might have said she had no mind at all; but so wise and right and tender a heart that it was as good as genius. This is to let you know what this little Pilgrim had been.

She rose up, and it was strange how like she felt to the child she remembered in that still summer morning so many years ago. Her little body, which had been worn and racked with pain, felt as light and unconscious of itself as then. She took her first step forward with the same sense of pleasure, yet of awe, suppressed delight and daring and wild adventure, yet perfect safety. But then the recollection of the little room in which she had fallen asleep came quickly, strangely over her, confusing her mind. "I must be dreaming, I suppose," she said to herself regretfully; for it was all so sweet that she wished it to be true. Her movement called her attention to herself, and she found that she was dressed, not in her night-dress, as she had lain down, but in a dress she did not know. She paused for a moment to look at it and wonder. She had never seen it before; she did not make out how it was made, or what stuff it was; but it fell so pleasantly about her, it was so soft and light, that in her confused state she abandoned that subject with only an additional sense of pleasure. And now the atmosphere became more distinct to her. She saw that under her feet was a greenness as of close velvet turf, both cool and warm, cool and soft to touch, but with no damp in it, as might have been at that early hour, and with flowers showing here and there. She stood looking round her, not able to identify the landscape because she was still confused a little, and then walked softly on, all the time afraid lest she should awake and lose the sweetness of it all, and the sense of rest and happiness. She felt so light, so airy, as if she could skim across the field like any child. It was bliss enough to breathe and move with every organ so free. After more than fifty years of hard service in the world to feel like this, even in a dream! She smiled to herself at her own pleasure; and then once more, yet more potently, there came back upon her the appearance of her room in which she had fallen asleep. How had she got from there to here? Had she been carried away in her sleep, or was it only a dream, and would she by and by find herself between the four dim walls again? Then this shadow of recollection faded away once more, and she moved forward, walking in a soft rapture over the delicious turf. Presently she came to a little mound upon which she paused to look about her. Every moment she saw a little farther: blue hills far away, extending in long sweet distance, an indefinite landscape, but fair and vast, so that there could be seen no end to it, not even the line of the horizon—save at one side, where there seemed to be a great shadowy gateway, and something dim beyond. She turned from the brightness to look at this, and when she had looked for some time she saw what pleased her still more, though she had been so happy before—people coming in. They were too far off for her to see clearly, but many came, each apart, one figure only at a time. To watch them amused her in the delightful leisure of her mind. Who were they? she wondered; but no doubt soon some of them would come this way, and she would see. Then suddenly she seemed to hear, as if in answer to her question, some one say, "Those who are coming in are the people who have died on earth." "Died!" she said to herself aloud, with a wondering sense of the inappropriateness of the word, which almost came the length of laughter. In this sweet air, with such a sense of life about, to suggest such an idea was almost ludicrous. She was so occupied with this that she did not look round to see who the speaker might be. She thought it over, amused, but with some new confusion of the mind. Then she said, "Perhaps I have died too," with a laugh to herself at the absurdity of the thought.

"Yes," said the other voice, echoing that gentle laugh of hers, "you have died too."

She turned round and saw another standing by her—a woman, younger and fairer and more stately than herself, but of so sweet a countenance that our little Pilgrim felt no shyness, but recognised a friend at once. She was more occupied looking at this new face, and feeling herself at once so much happier (though she had been so happy before) in finding a companion who could tell her what everything was, than in considering what these words might mean. But just then once more the recollection of the four walls, with their little pictures hanging, and the window with its curtains drawn, seemed to come round her for a moment, so that her whole soul was in a confusion. And as this vision slowly faded away (though she could not tell which was the vision, the darkened room or this lovely light), her attention came back to the words at which she had laughed, and at which the other had laughed as she repeated them. Died?—was it possible that this could be the meaning of it all.

"Died?" she said, looking with wonder in her companion's face, which smiled back to her. "But do you mean—? You cannot mean—? I have never been so well. I am so strong. I have no trouble anywhere. I am full of life."

The other nodded her beautiful head with a more beautiful smile, and the little Pilgrim burst out in a great cry of joy, and said—

"Is this all? Is it over?—is it all over? Is it possible that this can be all?"

"Were you afraid of it?" the other said. There was a little agitation for the moment in her heart. She was so glad, so relieved and thankful, that it took away her breath. She could not get over the wonder of it.

"To think one should look forward to it so long, and wonder and be even unhappy trying to divine what it will be—and this all!"

"Ah, but the angel was very gentle with you," said the young woman. "You were so tender and worn that he only smiled and took you sleeping. There are other ways; but it is always wonderful to think it is over, as you say."

The little Pilgrim could do nothing but talk of it, as one does after a very great event. "Are you sure, quite sure, it is so?" she said. "It would be dreadful to find it only a dream, to go to sleep again, and wake up—there—" This thought troubled her for a moment. The vision of the bedchamber came back, but this time she felt it was only a vision. "Were you afraid too?" she said, in a low voice.

"I never thought of it at all," the beautiful stranger said. "I did not think it would come to me; but I was very sorry for the others to whom it came, and grudged that they should lose the beautiful earth and life, and all that was so sweet."

"My dear!" cried the Pilgrim, as if she had never died, "oh, but this is far sweeter! and the heart is so light, and it is happiness only to breathe. Is it heaven here? It must be heaven."

"I do not know if it is heaven. We have so many things to learn. They cannot tell you everything at once," said the beautiful lady. "I have seen some of the people I was sorry for, and when I told them, we laughed—as you and I laughed just now—for pleasure."

"That makes me think," said the little Pilgrim. "If I have died as you say—which is so strange and me so living—if I have died, they will have found it out. The house will be all dark, and they will be breaking their hearts. Oh, how could I forget them in my selfishness, and be happy! I so lighthearted while they—"

She sat down hastily and covered her face with her hands and wept. The other looked at her for a moment, then kissed her for comfort and cried too. The two happy creatures sat there weeping together, thinking of those they had left behind, with an exquisite grief which was not unhappiness, which was sweet with love and pity. "And oh," said the little Pilgrim, "what can we do to tell them not to grieve? Cannot you send, cannot you speak—cannot one go to tell them?"

The heavenly stranger shook her head.

"It is not well, they all say. Sometimes one has been permitted; but they do not know you," she said, with a pitiful look in her sweet eyes. "My mother told me that her heart was so sick for me, she was allowed to go; and she went and stood by me, and spoke to me, and I did not know her. She came back so sad and sorry that they took her at once to our Father, and there, you know, she found that it was all well. All is well when you are there."

"Ah," said the little Pilgrim, "I have been thinking of other things—of how happy I was, and of *them*, but never of the Father—just as if I had not died."

The other smiled upon her with a wonderful smile.

"Do you think He will be offended—our Father? as if He were one of us?" she said.

And then the little Pilgrim, in her sudden grief to have forgotten Him, became conscious of a new rapture unexplainable in words. She felt His understanding to envelop her little spirit with a soft and clear penetration, and that nothing she did or said could ever be misconceived more. "Will you take me to Him?" she said, trembling yet glad, clasping her hands. And once again the other shook her head.

"They will take us both when it is time," she said. "We do not go at our own will. But I have seen our Brother—"

"Oh, take me to Him!" the little Pilgrim cried. "Let me see His face! I have so many things to say to Him. I want to ask him—Oh, take me to where I can see His face!"

And then once again the heavenly lady smiled.

"I have seen Him," she said. "He is always about—now here, now there. He will come and see you perhaps when you are not thinking—but when He pleases. We do not think here of what we will—"

The little Pilgrim sat very still, wondering at all this. She had thought when a soul left the earth that it went at once to God, and thought of nothing more except worship and singing of praises. But this was different from her thoughts. She sat and pondered and wondered. She was baffled at many points. She was not changed as she expected, but so much like herself still—still perplexed, and feeling herself foolish, not understanding, toiling after a something which she could not grasp. The only difference was that it was no trouble to her now. She smiled at herself, and at her dulness, feeling sure that by and by she would understand.

"And don't you wonder too?" she said to her companion, which was a speech such as she used to make upon the earth where people thought her little remarks disjointed, and did not always see the connection of them. But her friend of heaven knew what she meant.

"I do nothing but wonder," she said, "for it is all so natural—not what we thought."

"Is it long since you have been here?" the Pilgrim said.

"I came before you—but how long or how short I cannot tell, for that is not how we count. We count only by what happens to us. And nothing yet has happened to me, except that I have seen our Brother. My mother sees Him always. That means she has lived here a long time and well—"

"Is it possible to live ill—in heaven?" The little Pilgrim's eyes grew large as if they were going to have tears in them, and a little shadow seemed to come over her. But the other laughed softly and restored her confidence.

"I have told you I do not know if it is heaven or not. No one does ill, but some do little and some do much, just as it used to be. Do you remember in Dante there was a lazy spirit that stayed about the gates and never got farther? but perhaps you never read that."

"I was not clever," said the little Pilgrim, wistfully. "No, I never read it. I wish I had known more."

Upon which the beautiful lady kissed her again to give her courage, and said—

"It does not matter at all. It all comes to you whether you have known it or not."

"Then your mother came here long ago?" said the Pilgrim. "Ah, then I shall see my mother too."

"Oh, very soon—as soon as she can come; but there are so many things to do. Sometimes we can go and meet those who are coming, but it is not always so. I remember that she had a message. She could not leave her business, you may be sure, or she would have been here."

"Then you know my mother? Oh, and my dearest father too?"

"We all know each other," the lady said with a smile.

"And you? did you come to meet me—only out of kindness, though I do not know you?" the little Pilgrim said.

"I am nothing but an idler," said the beautiful lady, "making acquaintance. I am of little use as yet. I was very hard worked before I came here, and they think ft well that we should sit in the sun and take a little rest and find things out."

Then the little Pilgrim sat still and mused, and felt in her heart that she had found many things out. What she had heard had been wonderful, and it was more wonderful still to be sitting here all alone save for this lady, yet so happy and at ease. She wanted to sing, she was so happy, but remembered that she was old and had lost her voice, and then remembered again that she was no longer old, and perhaps had found it again. And then it occurred to her to remember how she had learned to sing, and how beautiful her sister's voice was, and how heavenly to hear her, which made her remember that this dear sister would be weeping, not singing, down where she had come from—and immediately the tears stood in her eyes.

"Oh," she said, "I never thought we should cry when we came here. I thought there were no tears in heaven."

"Did you think, then, that we were all turned into stone?" cried the beautiful lady. "It says, God shall wipe away all tears from our faces, which is not like saying there are to be no tears."

Upon which the little Pilgrim, glad that it was permitted to be sorry, though she was so happy, allowed herself to think upon the place she had so lately left. And she seemed to see her little room again with all the pictures hanging as she had left them, and the house darkened, and the dear faces she knew all sad and troubled; and to hear them saying over to each other all the little careless words she had said as if they were out of the Scriptures, and crying if any one but mentioned her name, and putting on crape and black dresses, and lamenting as if that which had happened was something very terrible. She cried at this and yet felt half inclined to laugh, but would not because it would be disrespectful to those she loved. One thing did not occur to her, and that was that they would be carrying her body, which she had left behind her, away to the grave. She did not think of this because she was not aware of the loss, and felt far too much herself to think that there was another part of her being buried in the ground. From this she was aroused by her companion asking her a question.

"Have you left many there?" she said.

"No one," said the little Pilgrim, "to whom I was the first on earth, but they loved me all the same; and if I could only, only let them know—"

"But I left one to whom I was the first on earth," said the other with tears in her beautiful eyes, "and oh, how glad I should be to be less happy if he might be less sad!"

"And you cannot go? you cannot go to him and tell him? Oh, I wish—" cried the little Pilgrim; but then she paused, for the wish died all away in her heart into a tender love for this poor sorrowful man whom she did not know. This gave her the sweetest pang she had ever felt, for she knew that all was well, and yet was so sorry, and would have willingly given up her happiness for his. All this the lady read in her eyes or her heart, and loved her for it; and they took hands and were silent together, thinking of those they had left, as we upon earth think of those who have gone from us, but only with far more understanding, and far greater love. "And have you never been able to do anything for him?" our Pilgrim said.

Then the beautiful lady's face flushed all over with the most heavenly warmth and light. Her smile ran over like the bursting out of the sun. "Oh, I will tell you," she said. "There was a moment when he was very sad and perplexed, not knowing what to think. There was something he could not understand; nor could I understand, nor did I know what it was until it was said to me, 'You may go and tell him.' And I went in the early morning, before he was awake, and kissed him, and said it in his ear. He woke up in a moment and understood, and everything was clear to him. Afterwards I heard him say, 'It is true that the night brings counsel. I had been troubled and distressed all day long, but in the morning it was quite clear to me.' And the other answered, 'Your brain was refreshed, and that made your judgment clear.' But they never knew it was I! That was a great delight. The dear souls! they are so foolish," she cried with the sweetest laughter that ran into tears. "One cries because one is so happy; it is a silly old habit," she said.

"And you were not grieved, it did not hurt you—that he did not know—"

"Oh, not then; not then! I did not go to him for that. When you have been here a little longer you will see the difference. When you go for yourself, out of impatience, because it still seems to you that you must know best, and they don't know you—then it strikes to your heart; but when you go to help them—ah," she cried, "when he comes how much I shall have to tell him! 'You thought it was sleep when it was I—when you woke so fresh and clear it was I that kissed you; you thought it your duty to me to be sad afterwards and were angry with yourself because you had wronged me of the first thoughts of your waking—when it was all me, all through!'"

"I begin to understand," said the little Pilgrim; "but why should they not see us, and why should not we tell them? It would seem so natural. If they saw us it would make them so happy, and so sure."

Upon this the lady shook her head.

"The worst of it is not that they are not sure—it is the parting. If this makes us sorry here, how can they escape the sorrow of it even if they saw us?—for we must be parted. We cannot go back to live with them, or why should we have died? And then we must all live our lives—they in their way, we in ours. We must not weigh them down, but only help them when it is seen that there is need for it. All this we shall know better by and by."

"You make it so clear, and your face is so bright," said our little Pilgrim gratefully. "You must have known a great deal, and understood even when you were in the world."

"I was as foolish as I could be," said the other, with her laugh that was as sweet as music; "yet thought I knew, and they thought I knew; but all that does not matter now."

"I think it matters, for look how much you have shown me; but tell me one thing more—how was it said to you that you must go and tell him? Was it some one who spoke—was it—"

Her face grew so bright that all the past brightness was as a dull sky to this. It gave out such a light of happiness that the little Pilgrim was dazzled.

"I was wandering about," she said, "to see this new place. My mother had come back between two errands she had, and had come to see me and tell me everything; and I was straying about wondering what I was to do, when suddenly I saw some one coming along, as it might be now—"

She paused and looked up, and the little Pilgrim looked up too with her heart beating, but there was no one. Then she gave a little sigh, and turned and listened again.

"I had not been looking for Him, or thinking. You

know my mind is too light. I am pleased with whatever is before me; and I was so curious, for my mother had told me many things: when suddenly I caught sight of Him passing by. He was going on, and when I saw this a panic seized me, lest He should pass and say nothing. I do not know what I did. I flung myself upon His robe, and got hold of it, or at least I think so. I was in such an agony lest He should pass and never notice me. But that was my folly. He pass! As if that could be!"

"And what did He say to you?" cried the little Pilgrim, her heart almost aching it beat so high with sympathy and expectation.

The lady looked at her for a little without saying anything.

"I cannot tell you," she said, "any more than I can tell if this is heaven. It is a mystery. When you see Him you will know. It will be all you have ever hoped for and more besides, for He understands everything. He knows what is in our hearts about those we have left, and why He sent for us before them. There is no need to tell Him anything; He knows. He will come when it is time; and after you have seen Him you will know what to do."

Then the beautiful lady turned her eyes towards the gate, and, while the little Pilgrim was still gazing, disappeared from her, and went to comfort some other stranger. They were dear friends always, and met often, but not again in the same way.

When she was thus left alone again, the little Pilgrim sat still upon the grassy mound, quite tranquil and happy, without wishing to move. There was such a sense of wellbeing in her that she liked to sit there and look about her, and breathe the delightful air, like the air of a summer morning, without wishing for anything.

"How idle I am!" she said to herself, in the very words

she had often used before she died; but then she was idle from weakness, and now from happiness. She wanted for nothing. To be alive was so sweet. There was a great deal to think about in what she had heard, but she did not even think about that, only resigned herself to the delight of sitting there in the sweet air and being happy. Many people were coming and going, and they all knew her, and smiled upon her, and those who were at a distance would wave their hands. This did not surprise her at all, for though she was a stranger, she, too, felt that she knew them all; but that they should be so kind was a delight to her which words could not tell. She sat and mused very sweetly about all that had been told her, and wondered whether she, too, might go sometimes, and, with a kiss and a whisper, clear up something that was dark in the mind of some one who loved her. "I that never was clever!" she said to herself, with a smile. And chiefly she thought of a friend whom she loved, who was often in great perplexity, and did not know how to guide herself amid the difficulties of the world.

The little Pilgrim half laughed with delight, and then half cried with longing to go, as the beautiful lady had done, and make something clear that had been dark before to this friend. As she was thinking what a pleasure it would be, some one came up to her, crossing over the flowery greenness, leaving the path on purpose. This was a being younger than the lady who had spoken to her before, with flowing hair all crisped with touches of sunshine, and a dress all white and soft, like the feathers of a white dove. There was something in her face different from that of the other, by which the little Pilgrim knew somehow, without knowing how, that she had come here as a child, and grown up in this celestial place. She was tall and fair, and came along with so musical a motion, as if her foot scarcely touched the ground, that she might have had wings. And the little Pilgrim indeed was not sure as she watched, whether it might not perhaps be an angel, for she knew that there were angels among the blessed people who were coming and going about, but had not been able yet to find one out. She knew that this newcomer was coming to her, and turned towards her with a smile and a throb at her heart of expectation. But when the heavenly maiden drew nearer, her face, though it was so fair, looked to the Pilgrim like another face, which she had known very well—indeed, like the homely and troubled face of the friend of whom she had been thinking. And so she smiled all the more, and held out her hands and said—"I am sure I know you," upon which the other kissed her, and said, "We all know each other; but I have seen you often before you came here," and knelt down by her, among the flowers that were growing, just in front of some tall lilies that grew over her, and made a lovely canopy over her head. There was something in her face that was like a child—her mouth so soft as if it had never spoken anything but heavenly words, her eyes brown and golden as if they were filled with light. She took the little Pilgrim's hands in hers, and held them and smoothed them between her own. These hands had been very thin and worn before, but now, when the Pilgrim looked at them, she saw that they became softer and whiter every moment with the touch of this immortal youth.

"I knew you were coming," said the maiden. "When my mother has wanted me I have seen you there. And you were thinking of her now—that was how I found you."

"Do you know, then, what one thinks?" said the little Pilgrim with wondering eyes.

"It is in the air; and when it concerns us it comes to us like the breeze. But we who are the children here, we feel it more quickly than you."

"Are you a child?" said the little Pilgrim, "or are you an angel? Sometimes you are like a child; but then your face shines and you are like—you must have some name for it here; there is nothing among the words I know." And then she paused a little, still looking at her, and cried, "Oh, if she could but see you, little Margaret! That would do her most good of all."

Then the maiden Margaret shook her lovely head. "What does her most good is the will of the Father," she said.

At this the little Pilgrim felt once more that thrill of expectation and awe. "Oh, child, you have seen Him?" she cried.

And the other smiled. "Have you forgotten who they are that always behold His face? We have never had any fear or trembling. We are not angels, and there is no other name; we are the children. There is something given to us beyond the others. We have had no other home."

"Oh, tell me, tell me!" the little Pilgrim cried.

Upon this Margaret kissed her, putting her soft cheek against hers, and said, "It is a mystery; it cannot be put into words; in your time you will know."

"When you touch me you change me, and I grow like you," the Pilgrim said. "Ah, if she could see us together, you and me! And will you go to her soon again? And do you see them always—what they are doing? and take care of them?"

"It is our Father who takes care of them, and our Lord who is our Brother. I do His errands when I am able. Sometimes He will let me go, sometimes another, according as it is best. Who am I that I should take care of them? I serve them when I may."

"But you do not forget them?" the Pilgrim said, with wistful eyes.

"We love them always," said Margaret. She was more still than the lady who had first spoken with the Pilgrim. Her countenance was full of a heavenly calm. It had never known passion nor anguish. Sometimes there was in it a far-seeing look of vision, sometimes the simplicity of a child. "But what are we in comparison? For He loves them more than we do. When He keeps us from them it is for love. We must each live our own life."

"But it is hard for them sometimes," said the little Pilgrim, who could not withdraw her thoughts from those she had left.

"They are never forsaken," said the angel-maiden.

"But oh! there are worse things than sorrow," the little Pilgrim said; "there is wrong, there is evil, Margaret. Will not He send you to step in before them, to save them from wrong?"

"It is not for us to judge," said the young Margaret, with eyes full of heavenly wisdom. "Our Brother has it all in His hand. We do not read their hearts like Him. Sometimes you are permitted to see the battle."

The little Pilgrim covered her eyes with her hands. "I could not—I could not! unless I knew they were to win the day."

"They will win the day in the end. But sometimes, when it was being lost, I have seen in His face a something—I cannot tell—more love than before. Something that seemed to say, 'My child, my child, would that I could do it for thee, my child!'"

"Oh! that is what I have always felt," cried the Pilgrim, clasping her hands; her eyes were dim, her heart for a moment almost forgot its blessedness. "But He could—Oh, little Margaret! He could! You have forgotten—Lord, if Thou wilt Thou canst—"

The child of heaven looked at her mutely, with sweet grave eyes, in which there was much that confused her who was a stranger here; and once more softly shook her head.

"Is it that He will not, then?" said the other with a low voice of awe. "Our Lord who died—He—"

"Listen," said the other, "I hear His step on the way."

The little Pilgrim rose up from the mound on which

she was sitting. Her soul was confused with wonder and fear. She had thought that an angel might step between a soul on earth and sin, and that if one but prayed and prayed, the dear Lord would stand between and deliver the tempted. She had meant when she saw His face to ask Him to save Was not He born, did not He live, and die to save? The angel-maiden looked at her all the while, with eyes that understood all her perplexity and her doubt, but spoke not. Thus it was that before the Lord came to her the sweetness of her first blessedness was obscured, and she found that here, too, even here, though in a moment she should see Him, there was need for faith. Young Margaret, who had been kneeling by her, rose up too and stood among the lilies, waiting, her soft countenance shining, her eyes turned towards Him who was coming. Upon her there was no cloud nor doubt. She was one of the children of that land familiar with His presence. And in the air there was a sound such as those who hear it alone can describe—a sound as of help coming and safety, like the sound of a deliverer when one is in deadly danger, like the sound of a conqueror, like the step of the dearest-beloved coming home. As it came nearer the fear melted away out of the beating heart of the Pilgrim. Who could fear so near Him? her breath went away from her, her heart out of her bosom, to meet His coming. Oh, never fear could live where He was! Her soul was all confused, but it was with hope and joy. She held out her hands in that amaze, and dropped upon her knees, not knowing what she did.

He was going about His Father's business, not lingering, yet neither making haste; and the calm and peace which the little Pilgrim had seen in the faces of the blessed were but reflections from the majestic gentleness of the countenance to which, all quivering with happiness and wonder, she lifted up her eyes. Many things there had been in her mind to say to Him. She wanted to ask for those she loved some things which perhaps He had over-looked. She wanted to say, "Send me." It seemed to her that here was the occasion she had longed for all her life. Oh, how many times had she wished to be able to go to Him, to fall at His feet, to show Him something which had been left undone, something which perhaps for her asking He would remember to do. But when this dream of her life was fulfilled, and the little Pilgrim kneeling, and all shaken and trembling with devotion and joy, was at His feet, lifting her face to Him, seeing Him, hearing Him—then she said nothing to Him at all. She no longer wanted to say anything, or wanted anything except what He chose, or had power to think of anything except that all was well, and everything—everything, as it should be in His hand. It seemed to her that all that she had ever hoped for was fulfilled when she met the look in His eyes. At first it seemed too bright for her to meet, but next moment she knew it was all that was needed to light up the world, and in it everything was clear. Her trembling ceased, her little frame grew inspired; though she still knelt, her head rose erect, drawn to Him like the flower to the sun. She could not tell how long it was, nor what was said, nor if it was in words. All that she knew was that she told Him all that ever she had thought, or wished, or intended in all her life, although she said nothing at all; and that He opened all things to her, and showed her that everything was well, and no one forgotten; and that the things she would have told Him of were more near His heart than hers, and those to whom she wanted to be sent were in His own hand. But whether this passed with words or without words she could not tell. Her soul expanded under His eyes like a flower. It opened out, it comprehended, and felt, and knew. She smote her hands together in her wonder that she could have missed seeing what was so clear, and laughed with a sweet scorn at her folly, as two people who love each other laugh at the little misunderstanding that has parted them. She was bold with Him, though she was so timid by nature, and ventured to laugh at herself, not to reproach herself—for His divine eyes spoke no blame, but smiled upon her folly too. And then He laid a hand upon her head, which seemed to fill her with currents of strength and joy running through all her veins. And then she seemed to come to herself saying loud out, "And that I will! and that I will!" and lo, she was kneeling on the warm soft sod alone, and hearing the sound of His footsteps as He went about His Father's business, filling all the air with echoes of blessing. And all the people who were coming and going smiled upon her, and she knew they were all glad for her that she had seen Him, and got the desire of her heart. Some of them waved their hands as they passed, and some paused a moment and spoke to her with tender congratulations. They seemed to have the tears in their eyes for joy, remembering every one the first time they had themselves seen Him, and the joy of it; so that all about there sounded a concord of happy thoughts all echoing to each other, "She has seen the Lord!"

Why did she say, "And that I will! and that I will!" with such fervour and delight? She could not have told but yet she knew. The first thing was that she had yet to wait and believe until all things should be accomplished, neither doubting nor fearing, but knowing that all should be well; and the second was that she must delay no longer, but rise up and serve the Father according to what was given her as her reward. When she had recovered a little of her rapture she rose from her knees, and stood still for a moment to be sure which way she was to go. And she was not aware what guided her, but yet turned her face in the appointed way without any doubt. For doubt was now gone away for ever, and that fear that once gave her so much trouble lest she might not be doing what was best. As she moved along she wondered at herself more and more. She felt no longer, as at first, like the child she remembered to have been, venturing out in the awful lovely stillness of the morning before any one was awake; but she felt that to move along was a delight, and that her foot scarcely touched the grass, and her whole being was instinct with such lightness of strength and life that it did not matter to her how far she went, nor what she carried, nor if the way was easy or hard. The way she chose was one of those which led to the great gate, and many met her coming from thence, with looks that were somewhat bewildered, as if they did not yet know whither they were going or what had happened to them. Upon whom she smiled as she passed them with soft looks of tenderness and sympathy, knowing what they were feeling, but did not stop to explain to them, because she had something else that had been given her to do. For this is what always follows in that country when you meet the Lord, that you instantly know what it is that He would have you do.

The little Pilgrim thus went on and on towards the gate, which she had not seen when she herself came through it, having been lifted in His arms by the great Death Angel, and set down softly inside, so that she did not know it, or even the shadow of it. As she drew nearer the light became less bright, though very sweet, like a lovely dawn, and she wondered to herself to think that she had been here but a moment ago, and yet so much had passed since then. And still she was not aware what was her errand, but wondered if she was to go back by these same gates, and perhaps return where she had been. She went up to them very closely, for she was curious to see the place through which she had come in her sleep, as a traveller goes back to see the city gate, with its bridge and portcullis, through which he has passed by night. The gate was very great, of a wonderful, curious architecture, and strange, delicate arches and canopies above. Some parts of them seemed cut very clean and clear; but the outlines were all softened with a sort of mist and shadow, so that it looked greater and higher than it was. The lower part was not one great doorway as the Pilgrim had supposed, but innumerable doors, all separate, and very narrow, so that but one could pass at a time, though the arch enclosed all, and seemed filled with great folding gates in which the smaller doors were set, so that if need arose a vast opening might be made for many to enter. Of the little doors many were shut as the Pilgrim approached; but from moment to moment, one after another would be pushed softly open from without, and some one would come in. The little Pilgrim looked at it all with great interest, wondering which of the doors she had herself come by; but while she stood absorbed by this, a door was suddenly pushed open close by her, and some one flung forward into the blessed country, falling upon the ground, and stretched out wild arms as though to clutch the very soil. This sight gave the Pilgrim a great surprise, for it was the first time she had heard any sound of pain, or seen any sight of trouble, since she entered here. In that moment she knew what it was that the dear Lord had given her to do. She had no need to pause to think, for her heart told her; and she did not hesitate as she might have done in the other life, not knowing what to say. She went forward, and gathered this poor creature into her arms, as if it had been a child, and drew her quite within the land of peace—for she had fallen across the threshold, so as to hinder any one entering who might be coming after her. It was a woman, and she had flung herself upon her face, so that it was difficult for the little Pilgrim to see what manner of person it was, for though she felt herself strong enough to take up this new-comer in her arms and carry her away, yet she forbore, seeing the will of the stranger was not so. For some time the woman lay moaning, with now and then a great sob shaking her as she lay. The little Pilgrim had taken her by both her arms, and drawn her head to rest upon her own lap, and was still holding the hands, which the poor creature had thrown out as if to clutch the ground. Thus she lay for a little while, as the little Pilgrim remembered she herself had lain, not wishing to move, wondering what had happened to her; and then she clutched the hands which grasped her, and said, muttering—

"You are some one new. Have you come to save me? Oh, save me! Oh, save me! Don't let me die!"

This was very strange to the little Pilgrim, and went to her heart. She soothed the stranger, holding her hands warm and light, and stooping over her.

"Dear," she said, "you must try and not be afraid."

"You say so," said the woman, "because you are well and strong. You don't know what it is to be seized in the middle of your life, and told that you've got to die. Oh, I have been a sinful creature! I am not fit to die. Can't you give me something that will cure me? What is the good of doctors and nurses if they cannot save a poor soul that is not fit to die?"

At this the little Pilgrim smiled upon her, always holding her fast, and said—

"Why are you so afraid to die?"

The woman raised her head to look who it was who put such a strange question to her.

"You are some one new," she said. "I have never seen you before. Is there anyone that is not afraid to die? Would *you* like to have to give your account all in a moment, without any time to prepare?"

"But you have had time to prepare," said the Pilgrim.

"Oh, only a very very little time; and I never thought it was true. I am not an old woman, and I am not fit to die; and I'm poor. Oh, if I were rich, I would bribe you to give me something to keep me alive. Won't you do it for pity?—won't you do it for pity? When you are as bad as I am, oh, you will perhaps call for some one to help you, and find nobody, like me."

"I will help you for love," said the little Pilgrim. "Some one who loves you has sent me."

The woman lifted herself up a little and shook her head. "There is nobody that loves me." Then she cast her eyes round her and began to tremble again (for the touch of the little Pilgrim had stilled her). "Oh, where am I?" she said. "They have taken me away; they have brought me to a strange place; and you are new. Oh, where have they taken me?—where am I?—where am I?" she cried. "Have they brought me here to die?"

Then the little Pilgrim bent over her and soothed her. "You must not be so much afraid of dying; that is all over. You need not fear that any more," she said, softly; "for here where you now are we have all died."

The woman started up out of her arms, and then she gave a great shriek that made the air ring, and cried out, "Dead! am I dead?" with a shudder and convulsion, throwing herself again wildly with outstretched hands upon the ground.

This was a great and terrible work for the little Pilgrim—the first she had ever had to do—and her heart failed her for a moment; but afterwards she remembered our Brother who sent her, and knew what was best. She drew closer to the new-comer and took her hand again.

"Try," she said, in a soft voice, "and think a little. Do you feel now so ill as you were? Do not be frightened, but think a little. I will hold your hand; and look at me; you are not afraid of me."

The poor creature shuddered again, and then she turned her face and looked doubtfully with great dark eyes dilated, and the brow and cheek so curved and puckered round them that they seemed to glow out of deep caverns. Her face was full of anguish and fear. But as she looked at the little Pilgrim her troubled gaze softened. Of her own accord she clasped her other hand upon the one that held hers, and then she said with a gasp—

"I am not afraid of you; that was not true that you said? You are one of the sisters, and you want to frighten me and make me repent?"

"You do repent," the Pilgrim said.

"Oh," cried the poor woman, "what has the like of you to do with me? Now I look at you I never saw any one that was like you before. Don't you hate me?—don't you loathe me? I do myself. It's so ugly to go wrong. I think now I would almost rather die and be done with it. You will say that is because I am going to get better. I feel a great deal better now. Do you think I am going to get over it? Oh, I am better! I could get up out of bed and walk about. Yes, but I am not in bed; where have you brought me? Never mind, it is a fine air; I shall soon get well here."

The Pilgrim was silent for a little, holding her hands. And then she said—

"Tell me how you feel now," in her soft voice.

The woman had sat up and was gazing round her. "It is very strange," she said; "it is all confused. I think upon my mother and the old prayers I used to say. For a long, long time I always said my prayers; but now I've got hardened, they say. Oh, I was once as fresh as any one. It all comes over me now. I feel as if I were young again—just come out of the country. I am sure that I could walk."

The little Pilgrim raised her up, holding her by her hands; and she stood and gazed round about her, making one or two doubtful steps. She was very pale, and the light was dim; her eyes peered into it with a scared yet eager look. She made another step, then stopped again.

"I am quite well," she said. "I could walk a mile. I could walk any distance. What was that you said? Oh, I tell you I am better! I am not going to die."

"You will never, never die," said the little Pilgrim; "are you not glad it is all over? Oh, I was so glad! And all the more you should be glad if you were so much afraid."

But this woman was not glad. She shrank away from her companion, then came close to her again, and gripped her with her hands.

"It is your fun," she said, "or just to frighten me; perhaps you think it will do me no harm as I am getting so well—you want to frighten me to make me good. But I mean to be good without that—I do! I do! When one is so near dying as I have been and yet gets better—for I am going to get better? Yes! you know it as well as I."

The little Pilgrim made no reply, but stood by looking at her charge, not feeling that anything was given her to say; and she was so new to this work that there was a little trembling in her lest she should not do everything as she ought. And the woman looked round with those anxious eyes gazing all about. The light did not brighten as it had done when the Pilgrim herself first came to this place. For one thing they had remained quite close to the gate, which no doubt threw a shadow. The woman looked at that, and then turned and looked into the dim morning, and did not know where she was, and her heart was confused and troubled.

"Where are we?" she said. "I do not know where it is; they must have brought me here in my sleep—where are we? How strange to bring a sick woman away out of her room in her sleep! I suppose it was the new doctor," she went on, looking very closely in the little Pilgrim's face, then paused, and, drawing a long breath, said softly, "It has done me good. It is better air—it is a new kind of cure."

But though she spoke like this, she did not convince herself; her eyes were wild with wondering and fear. She gripped the Pilgrim's arm more and more closely, and trembled, leaning upon her.

"Why don't you speak to me?" she said; "why don't you tell me? Oh, I don't know how to live in this place! What do you do?—how do you speak? I am not fit for it.

And what are you? I never saw you before nor any one like you. What do you want with me? Why are you so kind to me? Why—why—?"

And here she went off into a murmur of questions. Why? why? always holding fast by the little Pilgrim, always gazing round her, groping as it were in the dimness with her great eyes.

"I have come because our dear Lord, who is our Brother, sent me to meet you, and because I love you," the little Pilgrim said.

"Love me!" the woman cried, throwing up her hands, "but no one loves me. I have not deserved it." Here she grasped her close again with a sudden clutch, and cried out, "If this is what you say, where is God?"

"Are you afraid of Him?" the little Pilgrim said.

Upon which the woman trembled so that the Pilgrim trembled too with the quivering of her frame; then loosed her hold and fell upon her face, and cried—

"Hide me! Hide me! I have been a great sinner. Hide me that He may not see me," and with one hand tried to draw the Pilgrim's dress as a veil between her and something she feared.

"How should I hide you from Him who is everywhere? and why should I hide you from your Father?" the little Pilgrim said. This she said almost with indignation, wondering that any one could put more trust in her, who was no better than a child, than in the Father of all. But then she said, "Look in your heart and you will see you are not so much afraid as you think. This is how you have been accustomed to frighten yourself. But look now into your heart. You thought you were very ill at first, but not now; and you think you are afraid, but look in your heart—"

There was a silence, and then the woman raised her head with a wonderful look, in which there was amazement and doubt, as if she had heard some joyful thing but dared not yet believe that it was true. Once more she hid her face in her hands, and once more raised it again. Her eyes softened; a long sigh or gasp, like one taking breath after drowning, shook her breast. Then she said, "I think that is true. But if I am not afraid it is because I am—bad. It is because I am hardened. Oh, should not I fear Him who can send me away into—the lake that burns—into the pit—" And here she gave a great cry, but held the little Pilgrim all the while with her eyes, which seem to plead and ask for better news.

Then there came into the Pilgrim's heart what to say, and she took the woman's hand again and held it between her own. "That is the change," she said, "that comes when we come here. We are not afraid any more of our Father. We are not all happy. Perhaps you will not be happy at first. But if he says to you go—even to that place you speak of—you will know that it is well, and you will not be afraid. You are not afraid now—oh, I can see it in your eyes. You are not happy, but you are not afraid. You know it is the Father. Do not say God, that is far off—Father!" said the little Pilgrim, holding up the woman's hand clasped in her own. And there came into her soul an ecstasy, and tears that were tears of blessedness fell from her eyes, and all about her there seemed to shine a light. When she came to herself, the woman who was her charge had come quite close to her, and had added her other hand to that the Pilgrim held, and was weeping, and saying, "I am not afraid," with now and then a gasp and sob, like a child who, after a passion of tears, has been consoled, yet goes on sobbing and cannot quite forget, and is afraid to own that all is well again. Then the Pilgrim kissed her, and bade her rest a little, for even she herself felt shaken, and longed for a little quiet and to feel the true sense of the peace that was in her heart. She sat down beside her upon the ground, and made her lean her head against her shoulder, and thus they remained very still for a little time, saying no more. It seemed to the little Pilgrim that her companion had fallen asleep, and perhaps it was so, after so much agitation. All this time there had been people passing, entering by the many doors. And most of them paused a little to see where they were, and looked round them, then went on; and it seemed to the little Pilgrim that, according to the doors by which they entered, each took a different way. While she watched, another came in by the same door as that at which the woman who was her charge had come in. And he too stumbled and looked about him with an air of great wonder and doubt. When he saw her seated on the ground, he came up to her, hesitating as one in a strange place who does not want to betray that he is bewildered and has lost his way. He came with a little pretence of smiling, though his countenance was pale and scared, and said, drawing his breath quick, "I ought to know where I am, but I have lost my head, I think. Will you tell me which is the way?"

"What way?" cried the little Pilgrim, for her strength was gone from her, and she had no word to say to him. He looked at her with that bewilderment on his face, and said, "I find myself strange, strange. I ought to know where I am; but it is scarcely daylight yet. It is perhaps foolish to come out so early in the morning." This he said in his confusion, not knowing where he was, nor what he said.

"I think all the ways lead to our Father," said the little Pilgrim (though she had not known this till now). "And the dear Lord walks about them all. Here you never go astray."

Upon this the stranger looked at her, and asked in a faltering voice, "Are you an angel?" still not knowing what he said.

"Oh, no, no. I am only a Pilgrim," she replied.

"May I sit by you a little?" said the man. He sat down drawing long breaths as though he had gone through great fatigue; and looked about with wondering eyes. "You will wonder, but I do not know where I am," he said. "I feel as if I must be dreaming. This is not where I expected to come. I looked for something very different; do you think there can have been any mistake?"

"Oh, never that," she said; "there are no mistakes here."

Then he looked at her again, and said—

"I perceive that you belong to this country, though you say you are a pilgrim. I should be grateful if you would tell me Does one live here? And is this all? Is there no—no—? but I don't know what word to use. All is so strange, different from what I expected."

"Do you know that you have died?"

"Yes, yes, I am quite acquainted with that," he said, hurriedly, as if it had been an idea he disliked to dwell upon. "But then I expected—Is there no one to tell you where to go, or what you are to be—? or to take any notice of you?"

The little Pilgrim was startled by this tone. She did not understand its meaning, and she had not any word to say to him. She looked at him with as much bewilderment as he had shown when he approached her, and replied, faltering—

"There are a great many people here; but I have never heard if there is any one to tell you—"

"What does it matter how many people there are if you know none of them?" he said.

"We all know each other," she answered him; but then paused and hesitated a little, because this was what had been said to her, and of herself she was not assured of it, neither did she know at all how to deal with this stranger, to whom she had not any commission. It seemed that he had no one to care for him, and the little Pilgrim had a sense of compassion, yet of trouble, in her heart—for what could she say? And it was very strange to her to see one who was not content here.

"Ah, but there should be some one to point out the way, and tell us which is our circle, and where we ought to go," he said. And then he too was silent for a while, looking about him, as all were fain to do on their first arrival, finding everything so strange. There were people coming in at every moment, and some were met at the very threshold, and some went away alone, with peaceful faces; and there were many groups about, talking together in soft voices, but no one interrupted the other; and though so many were there, each voice was as clear as if it had spoken alone, and there was no tumult of sound as when many people assemble together in the lower world.

The little Pilgrim wondered to find herself with the woman resting upon her on one side, and the man seated silent on the other, neither having, it appeared, any guide but only herself who knew so little. How was she to lead them in the paths which she did not know?—and she was exhausted by the agitation of her struggle with the woman whom she felt to be her charge. But in this moment of silence she had time to remember the face of the Lord, when He gave her this commission, and her heart was strengthened. The man all this time sat and watched, looking eagerly all about him, examining the faces of those who went and came: and sometimes he made a little start as if to go and speak to some one he knew; but always drew back again and looked at the little Pilgrim, as if he had said, "This is the one who will serve me best." He spoke to her again after a while and said, "I suppose you are one of the guides that show the way."

"No," said the little Pilgrim, anxiously, "I know so little! It is not long since I came here. I came in the early morning—"

"Why, it is morning now. You could not come earlier than it is now. You mean yesterday."

"I think," said the Pilgrim, "that yesterday is the other

side; there is no yesterday here."

He looked at her with the keen look he had, to understand her the better; and then he said—

"No division of time! I think that must be monotonous. It will be strange to have no night; but I suppose one gets used to everything. I hope though there is something to do. I have always lived a very busy life. Perhaps this is just a little pause before we go—to be—to have—to get our—appointed place."

He had an uneasy look as he said this, and looked at her with an anxious curiosity, which the little Pilgrim did not understand.

"I do not know," she said softly, shaking her head. "I have so little experience. I have not been told of an appointed place."

The man looked at her very strangely.

"I did not think," he said, "that I should have found such ignorance here. Is it not well known that we must all appear before the judgment seat of God?"

These words seemed to cause a trembling in the still air, and the woman on the other side raised herself suddenly up, clasping her hands: and some of those who had just entered heard the words, and came and crowded about the little Pilgrim, some standing, some falling down upon their knees, all with their faces turned towards her. She who had always been so simple and small, so little used to teach; she was frightened with the sight of all these strangers crowding, hanging upon her lips, looking to her for knowledge. She knew not what to do or what to say. The tears came into her eyes.

"Oh," she said, "I do not know anything about a judgment seat. I know that our Father is here, and that when we are in trouble we are taken to Him to be comforted, and that our dear Lord our Brother is among us every day, and every one may see Him. Listen," she said, standing up suddenly among them, feeling strong as an angel. "I have seen Him; though I am nothing, so little as you see, and often silly, never clever as some of you are, I have seen Him! and so will all of you. There is no more that I know of," she said softly, clasping her hands. "When you see Him it comes into your heart what you must do."

And then there was a murmur of voices about her, some saying that was best, and some wondering if that were all, and some crying if He would but come now—while the little Pilgrim stood among them with her face shining, and they all looked at her, asking her to tell them more, to show them how to find Him. But this was far above what she could do, for she too was not much more than a stranger, and had little strength. She would not go back a step, nor desert those who were so anxious to know, though her heart fluttered almost as it had used to do before she died, what with her longing to tell them, and knowing that she had no more to say.

But in that land it is never permitted that one who stands bravely and fails not shall be left without succour; for it is no longer needful there to stand even to death, since all dying is over, and all souls are tested. When it was seen that the little Pilgrim was thus surrounded by so many that questioned her, there suddenly came about her many others from the brightness out of which she had come, who, one going to one hand, and one to another, safely led them into the ways in which their course lay: so that the Pilgrim was free to lead forth the woman who had been given her in charge, and whose path lay in a dim, but pleasant country, outside of that light and gladness in which the Pilgrim's home was.

"But," she said, "you are not to fear or be cast down, because He goes likewise by these ways, and there is not a corner in all this land but He is to be seen passing by; and He will come and speak to you, and lay His hand upon you; and afterwards everything will be clear, and you will know what you are to do."

"Stay with me till He comes—oh, stay with me," the woman cried, clinging to her arm.

"Unless another is sent," the little Pilgrim said. And it was nothing to her that the air was less bright there, for her mind was full of light, so that, though her heart still fluttered a little with all that had passed, she had no longing to return, nor to shorten the way, but went by the lower road sweetly, with the stranger hanging upon her, who was stronger and taller than she. Thus they went on, and the Pilgrim told her all she knew, and everything that came into her heart. And so full was she of the great things she had to say, that it was a surprise to her, and left her trembling, when suddenly the woman took away her clinging hand, and flew forward with arms outspread and a cry of joy. The little Pilgrim stood still to see, and on the path before them was a child, coming towards them singing, with a look such as is never seen but upon the faces of children who have come here early, and who behold the face of the Father, and have never known fear nor sorrow. The woman flew and fell at the child's feet, and he put his hand upon her, and raised her up, and called her "mother." Then he smiled upon the little Pilgrim, and led her away.

"Now she needs me no longer," said the Pilgrim; and it was a surprise to her, and for a moment she wondered in herself if it was known that this child should come so suddenly and her work be over; and also how she was to return again to the sweet place among the flowers from which she had come. But when she turned to look if there was any way, she found One standing by such as she had not yet seen. This was a youth, with a face just touched with manhood, as at the moment when the boy ends, when all is still fresh and pure in the heart; but he was taller and greater than a man.

"I am sent," he said, "little sister, to take you to the Father: because you have been very faithful, and gone beyond your strength."

And he took the little Pilgrim by the hand, and she knew he was an angel; and immediately the sweet air melted about them into light, and a hush came upon her of all thought and all sense, attending till she should receive the blessing, and her new name, and see what is beyond telling, and hear and understand:—

THE LITTLE PILGRIM
GOES UP HIGHER.

When the little Pilgrim came out of the presence of the Father, she found herself in the street of a great city. But what she saw and heard when she was with Him it is not given to the tongue of mortal to say, for it is beyond words, and beyond even thought. As the mystery of love is not to be spoken but to be felt, even in the lower earth, so, but much less, is that great mystery of the love of the Father to be expressed in words. The little Pilgrim was very happy when she went into that sacred place, but there was a great awe upon her, and it might even be said that she was afraid; but when she came out again she feared nothing, but looked with clear eyes upon all she saw, loving them, but no more overawed by them, having seen that which is above all. When she came forth again to her common life—for it is not permitted save for those who have attained the greatest heights to dwell there—she had no longer need of any guide, but came alone, knowing where to go, and walking where it pleased her, with reverence and a great delight in seeing and knowing all that was around, but no fear. It was a great city, but it was not like the great cities which she had seen. She understood as she passed along how it was that those who had been dazzled but by a passing glance had described the walls and the pavement as gold. They were like what gold is, beautiful and clear, of a lovely colour, but softer in tone than metal ever was, and as cool and fresh to walk upon and to touch as if they had been velvet grass. The buildings were all beautiful, of every style and form that it is possible to think of, yet in great harmony, as if every man had followed his own taste, yet all had been so combined and grouped by the master architect, that each individual feature enhanced the effect of the rest. Some of the houses were greater and some smaller, but all of them were rich in carvings and pictures and lovely decorations, and the effect was as if the richest materials had been employed, marbles and beautiful sculptured stone, and wood of beautiful tints, though the little Pilgrim knew that these were not like the marble and stone she had once known, but heavenly representatives of them, far better than they. There were people at work upon them, building new houses and making additions, and a great many painters painting upon them the history of the people who lived there, or of others who were worthy that commemoration. And the streets were full of pleasant sound, and of crowds going and coming, and the commotion of much business, and many things to do. And this movement, and the brightness of the air, and the wonderful things that were to be seen on every side, made the Pilgrim gay, so that she could have sung with pleasure as she went along. And all who met her smiled, and every group exchanged greetings as they passed along, all knowing each other. Many of them, as might be seen, had come there, as she did, to see the wonders of the beautiful city; and all who lived there were ready to tell them whatever they desired to know, and show them the finest houses and the greatest pictures. And this gave a feeling of holiday and pleasure which was delightful beyond description, for all the busy people about were full of sympathy with the strangers—bidding them welcome, inviting them into their houses, making the warmest fellowship. And friends were meeting continually on every side; but the Pilgrim had no sense that she was forlorn in being alone, for all were friends; and it pleased her to watch the others, and see how one turned this way and one another, every one finding something that delighted him above all other things. She herself took a great pleasure in watching a painter, who was standing upon a balcony a little way above her, painting upon a great fresco: and when he saw this he asked her to come up beside him and see his work. She asked him a great many questions about it, and why it was that he was working only at the draperies of the figures, and did not touch their faces, some of which were already finished and seemed to be looking at her, as living as she was, out of the wall, while some were merely outlined as yet. He told her that he was not a great painter to do this, or to design the great work, but that the master would come presently, who had the chief responsibility. "For we have not all the same genius," he said, "and if I were to paint this head it would not have the gift of life as that one has; but to stand by and see him put it in, you cannot think what a happiness that is: for one knows every touch, and just what effect it will have, though one could not do it one's self; and it is a wonder and a delight perpetual that it should be done."

The little Pilgrim looked up at him and said, "That is very beautiful to say. And do you never wish to be like him—to make the lovely, living faces as well as the other parts?"

"Is not this lovely too?" he said; and showed her how he had just put in a billowy robe, buoyed out with the wind, and sweeping down from the shoulders of a stately figure in such free and graceful folds that she would have liked to take it in her hand and feel the silken texture; and then he told her how absorbing it was to study the mysteries of colour and the differences of light. "There is enough in that to make one happy," he said. "It is thought by some that we will all come to the higher point with work and thought; but that is not my feeling; and whether it is so or not what does it matter, for our Father makes no difference: and all of us are necessary to everything that is done: and it is almost more delight to see the master do it than to do it with one's own hand. For one thing, your own work may rejoice you in your heart, but always with a little trembling, because it is never so perfect as you would have it—whereas in your master's work you have full content, because his idea goes beyond yours, and as he makes every touch you can feel 'that is right—that is complete—that is just as it ought to be.' Do you understand what I mean?" he said, turning to her with a smile.

"I understand it perfectly," she cried, clasping her hands together with the delight of accord. "Don't you think that is one of the things that are so happy here? you understand at half a word."

"Not everybody," he said, and smiled upon her like a brother; "for we are not all alike even here."

"Were you a painter?" she said, "in—in the other—?"

"In the old times. I was one of those that strove for the mastery, and sometimes grudged—We remember these things at times," he said gravely, "to make us more aware of the blessedness of being content."

"It is long since then?" she said with some wistfulness; upon which he smiled again.

"So long," he said, "that we have worn out most of our links to the world below. We have all come away, and those who were after us for generations. But you are a new-comer."

"And are they all with you? are you all together? do you live as in the old time?"

Upon this the painter smiled, but not so brightly as before.

"Not as in the old time," he said, "nor are they all here. Some are still upon the way, and of some we have no certainty, only news from time to time. The angels are very good to us. They never miss an occasion to bring us news; for they go everywhere, you know."

"Yes," said the little Pilgrim, though indeed she had not known it till now; but it seemed to her as if it had come to her mind by nature and she had never needed to be told.

"They are so tender-hearted," the painter said; "and

more than that, they are very curious about men and women. They have known it all from the beginning, and it is a wonder to them. There is a friend of mine, an angel, who is more wise in men's hearts than any one I know; and yet he will say to me sometimes, 'I do not understand you—you are wonderful.' They like to find out all we are thinking. It is an endless pleasure to them, just as it is to some of us to watch the people in the other worlds."

"Do you mean—where we have come from?" said the little Pilgrim.

"Not always there. We in this city have been long separated from that country, for all that we love are out of it."

"But not here?" the little Pilgrim cried again with a little sorrow—a pang that she had thought could never touch her again—in her heart.

"But coming! coming!" said the painter, cheerfully; "and some were here before us, and some have arrived since. They are everywhere."

"But some in trouble—some in trouble!" she cried, with the tears in her eyes.

"We suppose so," he said gravely; "for some are in that place which once was called among us the place of despair."

"You mean—" and though the little Pilgrim had been made free of fear, at that word which she would not speak, she trembled, and the light grew dim in her eyes.

"Well!" said her new friend, "and what then? The Father sees through and through it as He does here: they cannot escape Him: so that there is Love near them always. I have a son," he said, then sighed a little, but smiled again, "who is there."

The little Pilgrim at this clasped her hands with a piteous cry.

"Nay, nay," he said, "little sister; my friend I was telling you of, the angel, brought me news of him just now. Indeed there was news of him through all the city.

Did you not hear all the bells ringing? But perhaps that was before you came. The angels who know me best came one after another to tell me, and our Lord himself came to wish me joy. My son had found the way."

The little Pilgrim did not understand this, and almost thought that the painter must be mistaken or dreaming. She looked at him very anxiously and said—

"I thought that those unhappy—never came out any more."

The painter smiled at her in return, and said—

"Had you children in the old time?"

She paused a little before she replied.

"I had children in love," she said, "but none that were born mine."

"It is the same," he said; "it is the same; and if one of them had sinned against you, injured you, done wrong in any way, would you have cast him off, or what would you have done?"

"Oh!" said the little Pilgrim again, with a vivid light of memory coming into her face, which showed she had no need to think of this as a thing that might have happened, but knew. "I brought him home. I nursed him well again. I prayed for him night and day. Did you say cast him off? when he had most need of me? then I never could have loved him," she cried.

The painter nodded his head, and his hand with the pencil in it, for he had turned from his picture to look at her.

"Then you think you love better than our Father?" he said: and turned to his work, and painted a new fold in the robe, which looked as if a soft air had suddenly blown into it, and not the touch of a skilful hand.

This made the Pilgrim tremble, as though in her ignorance she had done something wrong. After that there came a great joy into her heart. "Oh, how happy you have made me!" she cried. "I am glad with all my heart for you and your son—" Then she paused a little and added, "But you said he was still there."

"It is true: for the land of darkness is very confusing, they tell me, for want of the true light, and our dear friends the angels are not permitted to help: but if one follows them, that shows the way. You may be in that land yet on your way hither. It was very hard to understand at first," said the painter; "there are some sketches I could show you. No one has ever made a picture of it, though many have tried; but I could show you some sketches—if you wish to see."

To this the little Pilgrim's look was so plain an answer that the painter laid down his pallet and his brush, and left his work, to show them to her as he had promised. They went down from the balcony and along the street until they came to one of the great palaces, where many were coming and going. Here they walked through some vast halls, where students were working at easels, doing every kind of beautiful work: some painting pictures, some preparing drawings, planning houses and palaces. The Pilgrim would have liked to pause at every moment to see one lovely thing or another, but the painter walked on steadily till he came to a room which was full of sketches, some of them like pictures in little, with many figures—some of them only a representation of a flower, or the wing of a bird. "These are all the master's," he said; "sometimes the sight of them will be enough to put something great into the mind of another. In this corner are the sketches I told you of." There' were two of them hanging together upon the wall, and at first it seemed to the little Pilgrim as if they represented the flames and fire of which she had read, and this made her shudder for the moment. But then she saw that it was a red light like a stormy sunset, with masses of clouds in the sky, and a low sun very fiery and dazzling, which no doubt to a hasty glance must have looked, with its dark shadows and high lurid lights, like the fires of the bottomless pit. But when you looked down you saw the reality what it was. The country that lay beneath was full of tropical foliage, but with many stretches of sand and dry plains, and in the foreground was a town, that looked very prosperous and crowded, though the figures were very minute, the subject being so great; but no one to see it would have taken it for anything but a busy and wealthy place, in a thunderous atmosphere, with a storm coming on. In the next there was a section of a street with a great banqueting hall open to the view, and many people sitting about the table. You could see that there was a great deal of laughter and conversation going on, some very noisy groups, but others that sat more quietly in corners and conversed, and some who sang, and every kind of entertainment. The little Pilgrim was very much astonished to see this, and turned to the painter, who answered her directly, though she had not spoken. "We used to think differently once. There are some who are there and do not know it. They think only it is the old life over again, but always worse, and they are led on in the ways of evil: but they do not feel the punishment until they begin to find out where they are and to struggle, and wish for other things."

The little Pilgrim felt her heart beat very wildly while she looked at this, and she thought upon the rich man in the parable, who, though he was himself in torment, prayed that his brother might be saved, and she said to herself, "Our dear Lord would never leave him there who could think of his brother when he was himself in such a strait." And when she looked at the painter he smiled upon her, and nodded his head. Then he led her to the other corner of the room where there were other pictures. One of them was of a party seated round a table and an angel looking on. The angel had the aspect of a traveller, as if he were passing quickly by, and had but paused a moment to look, when one of the men glancing up suddenly saw him. The picture was dim, but the startled look upon this man's face, and the sorrow on the angel's, appeared out of the misty background with such truth that the tears came into the little Pilgrim's eyes, and she said in her heart, "Oh, that I could go to him and help him!" The other sketches were dimmer and dimmer. You seemed to see out of the darkness gleaming lights, and companies of revellers, out of which here and there was one trying to escape. And then the wide plains in the night, and the white vision of the angel in the distance, and here and there by different paths a fugitive striving to follow. "Oh, sir," said the little Pilgrim, "how did you learn to do it? You have never been there."

"It was the master, not I; and I cannot tell you if he has ever been there. When the Father has given you that gift, you can go to many places, without leaving the one where you are. And then he has heard what the angels say."

"And will they all get safe at the last? and even that great spirit, he that fell from Heaven—"

The painter shook his head, and said, "It is not permitted to you and me to know such great things. Perhaps the wise will tell you if you ask them: but for me I ask the Father in my heart and listen to what He says."

"That is best!" the little Pilgrim said; and she asked the Father in her heart: and there came all over her such a glow of warmth and happiness that her soul was satisfied. She looked in the painter's face and laughed for joy. And he put out his hands as if welcoming some one, and his countenance shone; and he said—

"My son had a great gift. He was a master born, though it was not given to me. He shall paint it all for us so that the heart shall rejoice; and you will come again and see."

After that it happened to the little Pilgrim to enter into another great palace where there were many people reading, and some sitting at their desks and writing, and some consulting together, with many great volumes stretched out open upon the tables. One of these who was seated alone looked up as she paused, wondering at him, and smiled as every one did, and greeted her with such a friendly tone that the Pilgrim, who always had a great desire to know, came nearer to him and looked at the book, then begged his pardon, and said she did not know that books were needed here. And then he told her that he was one of the historians of the city where all the records of the world were kept, and that it was his business to work upon the great history, and to show what was the meaning of the Father in everything that had happened, and how each event came in its right place.

"And do you get it out of books?" she asked; for she was not learned, nor wise, and knew but little, though she always loved to know.

"The books are the records," he said; "and there are many here that were never known to us in the old days; for the angels love to look into these things, and they can tell us much, for they saw it; and in the great books they have kept there is much put down that was never in the books we wrote; for then we did not know. We found out about the kings and the state, and tried to understand what great purposes they were serving; but even these we did not know, for those purposes were too great for us, not knowing the end from the beginning; and the hearts of men were too great for us. We comprehended the evil sometimes, but never fathomed the good. And how could we know the lesser things which were working out God's way? for some of these even the angels did not know; and it has happened to me that our Lord Himself has come in sometimes to tell me of one that none of us had discovered."

"Oh," said the little Pilgrim, with tears in her eyes, "I should like to have been that one!—that was not known even to the angels, but only to Himself!"

The historian smiled. "It was my brother," he said.

The Pilgrim looked at him with great wonder. "Your brother, and you did not know him!"

And then he turned over the pages and showed her where the story was.

"You know," he said, "that we who live here are not of your time, but have lived and lived here till the old life is far away and like a dream. There were great tumults and fightings in our time, and it was settled by the prince of the place that our town was to be abandoned, and all the people left to the mercy of an enemy who had no mercy. But every day as he rode out he saw at one door a child, a little fair boy, who sat on the steps, and sang his little song like a bird. This child was never afraid of anything—when the horses pranced past him, and the troopers pushed him aside, he looked up into their faces and smiled. And when he had anything, a piece of bread, or an apple, or a plaything, he shared it with his playmates; and his little face, and his pretty voice, and all his pleasant ways, made that corner bright. He was like a flower growing there; everybody smiled that saw him."

"I have seen such a child," the little Pilgrim said.

"But we made no account of him," said the historian. "The Lord of the place came past him every day, and always saw him singing in the sun by his father's door. And it was a wonder then, and it has been a wonder ever since, why, having resolved upon it, that prince did not abandon the town, which would have changed all his fortune after. Much had been made clear to me since I began to study, but not this: till the Lord Himself came to me and told me. The prince looked at the child till he loved him, and he reflected how many children there were like this that would be murdered, or starved to death, and he could not give up the little singing boy to the sword. So he remained; and the town was saved, and he became a great king. It was so secret that even the angels did not know it. But without that child the history would not have been complete."

"And is he here?" the little Pilgrim said.

"Ah," said the historian, "that is more strange still; for that which saved him was also to his harm. He is not here. He is—elsewhere."

The little Pilgrim's face grew sad; but then she remembered what she had been told.

"But you know," she said, "that he is coming?"

"I know that our Father will never forsake him, and that everything that is being accomplished in him is well."

"Is it well to suffer? Is it well to live in that dark stormy country? Oh, that they were all here, and happy like you!"

He shook his head a little and said—

"It was a long time before I got here; and as for suffering that matters little. You get experience by it. You are more accomplished and fit for greater work in the end. It is not for nothing that we are permitted to wander: and sometimes one goes to the edge of despair—"

She looked at him with such wondering eyes that he answered her without a word.

"Yes," he said, "I have been there."

And then it seemed to her that there was something in his eyes which she had not remarked before. Not only the great content that was everywhere, but a deeper light, and the air of a judge who knew both good and evil, and could see both sides, and understood all, both to love and to hate.

"Little sister," he said, "you have never wandered far—it is not needful for such as you. Love teaches you, and you need no more; but when we have to be trained for an office like this, to make the way of the Lord clear through all the generations, reason is that we should see everything, and learn all that man is and can be. These things are too deep for us; we stumble on, and know not till after. But now to me it is all clear."

She looked at him again and again while he spoke, and it seemed to her that she saw in him such great knowledge and tenderness as made her glad; and how he could understand the follies that men had done, and fathom what real meaning was in them, and disentangle all the threads. He smiled as she gazed at him, and answered as if she had spoken.

"What was evil perishes, and what was good remains; almost everywhere there is a little good. We could not understand all if we had not seen all and shared all."

"And the punishment too," she said, wondering more and more.

He smiled so joyfully that it was like laughter.

"Pain is a great angel," he said. "The reason we hated him in the old days was because he tended to death and decay; but when it is towards life he leads, we fear him no more. The welcome thing of all in the land of darkness is when you see him first and know who he is: for by this you are aware that you have found the way."

The little Pilgrim did nothing but question with her anxious eyes, for this was such a wonder to her, and she could not understand. But he only sat musing with a smile over the things he remembered. And at last he said—

"If this is so interesting to you, you shall read it all in another place, in the room where we have laid up our own experiences, in order to serve for the history afterwards. But we are still busy upon the work of the earth. There is always something new to be discovered. And it is essential for the whole world that the chronicle should be full. I am in great joy because it was but just now that our Lord told me about that child. Everything was imperfect without him, but now it is clear."

"You mean your brother? And you are happy though you are not sure if he is happy?" the little Pilgrim said.

"It is not to be happy that we live," said he; and then,

"We are all happy so soon as we have found the way."

She would have asked him more, but that he was called to a consultation with some others of his kind, and had to leave her, waving his hand to her with a tender kindness, which went to her heart. She looked after him with great respect, and almost awe; for it seemed to her that a man who had been in the land of darkness, and made his way out of it, must be more wonderful than any other. She looked round for a little upon the great library, full of all the books that had ever been written, and where people were doing their work, examining and reading and making extracts, every one with looks of so much interest, that she almost envied them—though it was a generous delight in seeing people so happy in their occupation, and a desire to associate herself somehow in it, rather than any grudging of their satisfaction that was in her mind. She went about all the courts of this palace alone, and everywhere saw the same work going on, and everywhere met the same kind looks. Even when the greatest of all looked up from his work and saw her, he would give her a friendly greeting and a smile; and nobody was too wise to lend an ear to the little visitor, or to answer her questions. And this was how it was that she began to talk to another, who was seated at a great table with many more, and who drew her to him by something that was in his looks, though she could not have told what it was. It was not that he was kinder than the rest, for they were all kind. She stood by him a little, and saw how he worked and would take something from one book and something from another, putting them ready for use. And it did not seem any trouble to do this work, but only pleasure, and the very pen in his hand was like a winged thing, as if it loved to write. When he saw her watching him, he looked up and showed her the beautiful book out of which he was copying, which was all illuminated with lovely pictures.

"This is one of the volumes of the great history," he said. "There are some things in it which are needed for another, and it is a pleasure to work at it. If you will come here you will be able to see the page while I write."

Then the little Pilgrim asked him some questions about the pictures, and he answered her, describing and explaining them; for they were in the middle of the history, and she did not understand what it was. When she said, "I ought not to trouble you, for you are busy," he smiled so kindly, that she smiled too for pleasure. And he said—

"There is no trouble here. When we are not allowed to work, as sometimes happens, that makes us not quite so happy, but it is very seldom that it happens so."

"Is it for punishment?" she said.

And then he laughed out with a sound which made all the others look up smiling; and if they had not all looked so tenderly at her, as at a child who has made such a mistake as it is pretty for the child to make, she would have feared she had said something wrong; but she only laughed at herself too, and blushed a little, knowing that she was not wise: and to put her at her ease again, he turned the leaf and showed her other pictures, and the story which went with them, from which he was copying something. And he said—

"This is for another book, to show how the grace of the Father was beautiful in some homes and families. It is not the great history, but connected with it: and there are many who love that better than the story which is more great."

Then the Pilgrim looked in his face and said—

"What I want most is, to know about your homes here."

"It is all home here," he said, and smiled; and then, as he met her wistful looks, he went on to tell her that he and his brothers were not always there. "We have all our occupations," he said, "and sometimes I am sent to inquire into facts that have happened, of which the record is not clear; for we must omit nothing; and sometimes we are told to rest and take in new strength; and sometimes—"

"But oh, forgive me," cried the little Pilgrim, "you had some who were more dear to you than all the world in the old time?"

And the others all looked up again at the question, and looked at her with tender eyes, and said to the man whom she questioned, "Speak!"

He made a little pause before he spoke, and he looked at one here and there, and called to them—

"Patience, brother," and "Courage, brother." And then he said, "Those whom we loved best are nearly all with us; but some have not yet come."

"Oh," said the little Pilgrim, "but how then do you bear it, to be parted so long—so long?"

Then one of those to whom the first speaker had called out "Patience" rose, and came to her smiling; and he said—

"I think every hour that perhaps she will come, and the joy will be so great, that thinking of that makes the waiting short: and nothing here is long, for it never ends; and it will be so wonderful to hear her tell how the Father has guided her, that it will be a delight to us all; and she will be able to explain many things, not only for us, but for all; and we love each other so, that this separation is as nothing in comparison with what is to come."

It was beautiful to hear this, but it was not what the little Pilgrim expected, for she thought they would have told her of the homes to which they all returned when their work was over, and a life which was like the life of the old time; but of this they said nothing, only looking at her with smiling eyes, as at the curious questions of a child. And there were many other things she would have asked, but refrained when she looked at them, feeling as if she did not yet understand; when one of them broke forth suddenly in a louder voice, and said—

"The little sister knows only the little language and the beginning of days. She has not learned the mysteries, and what Love is, and what life is."

And another cried, "It is sweet to hear it again;" and they all gathered round her with tender looks, and began to talk to each other, and tell her, as men will tell of the games of their childhood, of things that happened, which were half forgotten, in the old time.

After this the little Pilgrim went out again into the beautiful city, feeling in her heart that everything was a mystery, and that the days would never be long enough to learn all that had yet to be learned, but knowing now that this, too, was the little language, and pleased with the sweet thought of so much that was to come. For one had whispered to her as she went out that the new tongue, and every explanation, as she was ready for it, would come to her through one of those whom she loved best, which is the usage of that country. And when the stranger has no one there that is very dear, then it is an angel who teaches the greater language, and this is what happens often to the children who are brought up in that heavenly place. When she reached the street again, she was so pleased with this thought that it went out of her mind to ask her way to the great library, where she was to read the story of the historian's journey through the land of darkness; indeed she forgot that land altogether, and thought only of what was around her in the great city which is beyond everything that eye has seen, or that ear has heard, or that it has entered into the imagination to conceive. And now it seemed to her that she was much more familiar with the looks of the people, and could distinguish between those who belonged to the city, and those who were visitors like herself; and also could tell which they were who had entered into the mysteries of the kingdom, and which were, like herself, only acquainted with the beginning of days. And it came to her mind—she could not tell how—that it was best not to ask questions, but to wait until the beloved one should come, who would teach her the first words. For in the meantime she did not feel at all impatient or disturbed by her want of knowledge, but laughed a little at herself to suppose that she could find out everything, and went on looking round her, and saying a word to every one she met, and enjoying the holiday looks of all the strangers, and the sense she had in her heart of holiday too. She was walking on in this pleasant way, when she heard a sound that was like silver trumpets, and saw the crowd turn towards an open space in which all the beautiful buildings were shaded with fine trees, and flowers were springing at the very edge of the pavements. The strangers all hastened along to hear what it was, and she with them, and some also of the people of the place. And as the little Pilgrim found herself walking by a woman who was of these last, she asked her what it was.

And the woman told her it was a poet who had come to say to them what had been revealed to him, and that the two with the silver trumpets were angels of the musicians' order, whose office it was to proclaim everything that was new, that the people should know. And many of those who were at work in the palaces came out and joined the crowd, and the painter who had showed the little Pilgrim his picture, and many whose faces she began to be acquainted with. The poet stood up upon a beautiful pedestal all sculptured in stone, and with wreaths of living flowers hung upon it—and when the crowd had gathered in front of him, he began his poem. He told them that it was not about this land, or anything that happened in it, which they knew as he did, but that it was a story of the old time, when men were walking in darkness, and when no one knew the true meaning even of what he himself did, but had to go on as if blindly, stumbling and groping with their hands. And, "Oh, brethren," he said, "though all is more beautiful and joyful here where we know, yet to remember the days when we knew not, and the ways when all was uncertain, and the end could not be distinguished from the beginning, is sweet and dear; and that which was done in the dim twilight should be celebrated in the day; and our Father Himself loves to hear of those who, having not seen, loved, and who learned without any teacher, and followed the light, though they did not understand."

And then he told them the story of one who had lived in the old time; and in that air, which seemed to be made of sunshine, and amid all those stately palaces, he described to them the little earth which they had left behind—the skies that were covered with clouds, and the ways that were so rough and stony, and the cruelty of the oppressor, and the cries of those that were oppressed. And he showed the sickness and the troubles, and the sorrow and danger; and how death stalked about, and tore heart from heart; and how sometimes the strongest would fail, and the truest fall under the power of a lie, and the tenderest forget to be kind; and how evil things lurked in every corner to beguile the dwellers there; and how the days were short and the nights dark, and life so little that by the time a man had learned something it was his hour to die. "What can a soul do that is born there?" he cried; "for war is there and fighting, and perplexity and darkness; and no man knows if that which he does will be for good or evil, or can tell which is the best way, or know the end from the beginning; and those he loves the most are a mystery to him, and their thoughts beyond his reach. And clouds are between him and the Father, and he is deceived with false gods and false teachers, who make him to love a lie." The people who were listening held their breath, and a shadow like a cloud fell on them, and they remembered and knew that it was true. But the next moment their hearts rebelled, and one and another would have spoken, and the little Pilgrim herself had almost cried out and made her plea for the dear earth which she loved: when he suddenly threw forth his voice again like a great song. "Oh, dear mother earth," he cried; "oh, little world and great, forgive thy son! for lovely thou art and dear, and the sun of God shines upon thee and the sweet dews fall; and there were we born, and loved, and died, and are come hence to bless the Father and the Son. For in no other world, though they are so vast, is it given to any to know the Lord in the darkness, and follow Him groping, and make way through sin and death, and overcome the evil, and conquer in His Name." At which there was a great sound of weeping and of triumph, and the little Pilgrim could not contain herself, but cried out too in joy as if for a deliverance. And then the poet told his tale. And as he told them of the man who was poor and sorrowful and alone, and how he loved and was not loved again, and trusted and was betrayed, and was tempted and drawn into the darkness, so that it seemed as if he must perish; but, when hope was almost gone, turned again from the edge of despair, and confronted all his enemies, and fought and conquered, the people followed every word with great outcries of love and pity and wonder. For each one as he listened remembered his own career and that of his brethren in the old life, and admired to think that all the evil was past, and wondered how, out of such tribulation and through so many dangers, all were safe and blessed here. And there were others that were not of them, who listened, some seated at the windows of the palaces and some standing in the great square—people who were not like the others, whose bearing was more majestic, and who looked upon the crowd all smiling and weeping with wonder and interest, but had no knowledge of the cause, and listened as it were to a tale that is told. The poet and his audience were as one, and at every period of the story there was a deep breathing and pause, and every one looked at his neighbour, and some grasped each other's hands as they remembered all that was in the past; but the strangers listened and gazed and observed all, as those who listen and are instructed in something beyond their knowledge. The little Pilgrim stood all this time not knowing where she was, so intent was she upon the tale, and as she listened it seemed to her that all her own life was rolling out before her, and she remembered the things that had been, and perceived how all had been shaped and guided, and trembled a little for the brother who was in danger, yet knew that all would be well.

The woman who had been at her side listened too with all her heart, saying to herself as she stood in the crowd, "He has left nothing out! The little days they were so short, and the skies would change all in a moment and one's heart with them. How he brings it all back!" And she put up her hand to dry away a tear from her eyes, though her face all the time was shining with the recollection. The little Pilgrim was glad to be by the side of a woman after talking with so many men, and she put out her hand and touched the cloak that this lady wore, and which was white and of the most beautiful texture, with gold threads woven in it, or something that looked like gold.

"Do you like," she said, "to think of the old time?"

The woman turned and looked down upon her, for she was tall and stately, and immediately took the hand of the little Pilgrim into hers, and held it without answering, till the poet had ended and come down from the place where he had been standing. He came straight through the crowd to where this lady stood, and said something to her. "You did well to tell me," looking at her with love in his eyes—not the tender sweetness of all those kind looks around, but the love that is for one. The little Pilgrim looked at them with her heart beating, and was very glad for them, and happy in herself, for she had not seen this love before since she came into the city, and it had troubled her to think that perhaps it did not exist any more. "I am glad," the lady said, and gave him her other hand; "but here is a little sister who asks me something, and I must answer her. I think she has but newly come."

"She has a face full of the morning," the poet said. It did the little Pilgrim good to feel the touch of the warm, soft hand, and she was not afraid, but lifted her eyes and spoke to the lady, and to the poet. "It is beautiful what you said to us. Sometimes in the old time we used to look up to the beautiful skies and wonder what there was above the clouds, but we never thought that up here in this great city you would be thinking of what we were doing, and making beautiful poems all about us. We thought that you would sing wonderful psalms, and talk of things high, high above us."

"The little sister does not know what the meaning of the earth is," the poet said. "It is but a little speck, but it is the centre of all. Let her walk with us, and we will go home, and you will tell her, Ama, for I love to hear you talk."

"Will you come with us?" the lady said.

And the little Pilgrim's heart leaped up in her, to think she was now going to see a home in this wonderful city; and they went along hand in hand, and though they were three together, and many were coming and going, there was no difficulty, for every one made way for them. And there was a little murmur of pleasure as the poet passed, and those who had heard his poem made obeisance to him, and thanked him, and thanked the Father for him, that he was able to show them so many beautiful things. And they walked along the street which was shining with colour, and saw, as they passed, how the master painter had come to his work, and was standing upon the balcony where the little Pilgrim had been, and bringing out of the wall, under his hand, faces which were full of life, and which seemed to spring forth as if they had been hidden there. "Let us wait a little and see him working," the poet said: and all round about the people stopped on their way, and there was a soft cry of pleasure and praise all through the beautiful street. And the painter with whom the little Pilgrim had talked before came, and stood behind her as if he had been an old friend, and called out to her at every new touch to mark how this and that was done. She did not understand as he did, but she saw how beautiful it was, and she was glad to have seen the great painter, as she had been glad to hear the great poet. It seemed to the little Pilgrim as if everything happened well for her, and that no one had ever been so blessed before. And to make it all more sweet, this new friend, this great and sweet lady, always held her hand, and pressed it softly when something more lovely appeared; and even the pictured faces on the wall seemed to beam upon her, as they came out one by one like the stars in the sky. Then the three went on again, and passed by many more beautiful palaces, and great streets leading away into the light, till you could see no farther; and they met with bands of singers, who sang so sweetly that the heart seemed to leap out of the Pilgrim's breast to meet with them, for above all things this was what she had loved most. And out of one of the palaces there came such glorious music, that everything she had seen and heard before seemed as nothing in comparison. And amid all these delights they went on and on, but without wearying, till they came out of the streets into lovely walks and alleys, and made their way to the banks of a great river, which seemed to sing too, a soft melody of its own.

And here there were some fair houses surrounded by gardens and flowers that grew everywhere, and the doors were all open, and within everything was lovely and still, and ready for rest if you were weary. The little Pilgrim was not weary, but the lady placed her upon a couch in the porch, where the pillars and the roof were all formed of interlacing plants and flowers; and there they sat with her and talked, and explained to her many things. They told her that the earth, though so small, was the place in all the world to which the thoughts of those above were turned. "And not only of us who have lived there, but of all our brothers in the other worlds; for we are the race which the Father has chosen to be the example. In every age there is one that is the scene of the struggle and the victory, and it is for this reason that the chronicles are made, and that we are all placed here to gather the meaning of what has been done among men. And I am one of those," the lady said, "that go back to the dear earth and gather up the tale of what our little brethren are doing. I have not to succour, like some others, but only to see and bring the news; and he makes them into great poems as you have heard; and sometimes the master painter will take one and make of it a picture; and there is nothing that is so delightful to us as when we can bring back the histories of beautiful things."

"But, oh," said the little Pilgrim, "what can there be on earth so beautiful as the meanest thing that is here?"

Then they both smiled upon her and said, "It is more beautiful than the most beautiful thing here to see how, under the low skies and in the short days, a soul will turn to our Father. And sometimes," said Ama, "when I am watching, one will wander and stray, and be led into the dark till my heart is sick; then come back and make me glad. Sometimes I cry out within myself to the Father, and say, 'Oh, my Father, it is enough!' and it will seem to me that it is not possible to stand by and see his destruction. And then while you are gazing, while you are crying, he will recover and return, and go on again. And to the angels it is more wonderful than to us, for they have never lived there. And all the other worlds are eager to hear what we can tell them. For no one knows except the

Father how the battle will turn, or when it will all be accomplished; and there are some who tremble for our little brethren. For to look down and see how little light there is, and how no one knows what may happen to him next, makes them afraid who never were there."

The little Pilgrim listened with an intent face, clasping her hands, and said—"But it never could be that our Father should be overcome by evil. Is not that known in all the worlds?"

Then the lady turned and kissed her: and the poet broke forth in singing, and said, "Faith is more heavenly than heaven; it is more beautiful than the angels. It is the only voice that can answer to our Father. We praise Him, we glorify Him, we love His name, but there is but one response to Him through all the worlds, and that is the cry of the little brothers, who see nothing and know nothing, but believe that He will never fail."

At this the little Pilgrim wept, for her heart was touched: but she said—"We are not so ignorant: for we have our Lord who is our Brother, and He teaches us all that we require to know."

Upon this the poet rose and lifted up his hands and spoke once more; but it was as if he spoke to others, to some one at a distance; it was in the other language which the little Pilgrim still did not understand, but she could make out that it sounded like a great proclamation that He was wise as He was good, and called upon all to see that the Lord had chosen the only way. And the sound of the poet's voice was like a great trumpet sounding bold and sweet, as if to tell this to those who were far away.

"For you must know," said the Lady Ama, who all the time held the Pilgrim's hand, "that it is permitted to all to judge according to the wisdom that has been given them. And there are some who think that our dear Lord might have found another way, and that wait, sometimes with trembling, lest He should fail; but not among us who have lived on earth, for we know. And it is our work to show to all the worlds that His way never fails, and how wonderful it is, and beautiful above all that heart has conceived. And thus we justify the ways of God, who is our Father. But in the other worlds there are many who will continue to fear until the history of the earth is all ended and the chronicles are made complete."

"And will that be long?" the little Pilgrim cried, feeling in her heart that she would like to go to all the worlds and tell them of our Lord, and of His love, and how the thought of Him makes you strong; and it troubled her a little to hear her friends speak of the low skies and the short days, and the dimness of that dear country which she had left behind, in which there were so many still whom she loved.

Upon this Ama shook her head, and said that of that day no one knew, not even our Lord, but only the Father: and then she smiled and answered the little Pilgrim's thought. "When we go back," she said, "it is not as when we lived there; for now we see all the dangers of it and the mysteries which we did not see before. It was by the Father's dear love that we did not see what was around us and about us while we lived there, for then our hearts would have fainted: and that makes us wonder now that any one endures to the end."

"You are a great deal wiser than I am," said the little Pilgrim; "but though our hearts had fainted how could we have been overcome? for He was on our side."

At this neither of them made any reply at first, but looked at her; and at length the poet said that she had brought many thoughts back to his mind, and how he had himself been almost worsted when one like her came to him and gave strength to his soul. "For that He was on our side was the only thing she knew," he said, "and all that could be learned or discovered was not worthy of naming beside it. And this I must tell when next I speak to the people, and how our little sister brought it to my mind."

And then they paused from this discourse, and the little Pilgrim looked round upon the beautiful houses and the fair gardens, and she said—

"You live here? and do you come home at night? but I do not mean at night, I mean when your work is done. And are they poets like you that dwell all about in these pleasant places, and the—"

She would have said the children, but stopped, not knowing if perhaps it might be unkind to speak of the children when she saw none there.

Upon this the lady smiled once more, and said—

"The door stands open always, so that no one is shut out, and the children come and go when they will. They are children no longer, and they have their appointed work like him and me."

"And you are always among those you love?" the Pilgrim said; upon which they smiled again and said, "We all love each other;" and the lady held her hand in both of hers, and caressed it, and softly laughed, and said, "You know only the little language. When you have been taught the other you will learn many beautiful things."

She rested for some time after this, and talked much with her new friends: and then there came into the heart of the little Pilgrim a longing to go to the place which was appointed for her, and which was her home, and to do the work which had been given her to do. And when the lady saw this she rose and said that she would accompany her a little upon her way. But the poet bade her farewell and remained under the porch, with the green branches shading him, and the flowers twining round the pillars, and the open door of his beautiful house behind him. When she looked back upon him he waved his hand to her as if bidding her God-speed, and the lady by her side looked back too and waved her hand, and the little Pilgrim felt tears of happiness come to her eyes; for she had been wondering with a little disappointment to see that the people in the city, except those who were strangers, were chiefly alone, and not like those in the old world where the husband and wife go together. It consoled her to see again two who were one. The lady pressed her hand in answer to her thought, and bade her pause a moment and look back into the city as they passed the end of the great street out of which they came. And then the Pilgrim was more and more consoled, for she saw many who had before been alone now walking together hand in hand.

"It is not as it was," Ama said. "For all of us have work to do which is needed for the worlds, and it is no longer needful that one should sit at home while the other goes forth; for our work is not for our life as of old, or for ourselves, but for the Father who has given us so great a trust. And, little sister, you must know that though we are not so great as the angels, nor as many that come to visit us from the other worlds, yet we are nearer to Him. For we are in His secret, and it is ours to make it clear."

The little Pilgrim's heart was very full to hear this; but she said—

"I was never clever, nor knew much. It is better for me to go away to my little border-land, and help the strangers who do not know the way."

"Whatever is your work is the best," the lady said; "but though you are so little you are in the Father's secret too; for it is nature to you to know what the others cannot be sure of, that we must have the victory at the last. So that we have this between us, the Father and we. And though all are His children, we are of the kindred of God, because of our Lord who is our Brother;" and then the Lady Ama kissed her, and bade her when she returned to the great city, either for rest or for love, or because the Father sent for her, that she should come to the house by the river. "For we are friends for ever," she said, and so threw her white veil over her head, and was gone upon her mission, whither the little Pilgrim did not know.

And now she found herself at a distance from the great city which shone in the light with its beautiful towers, and roofs, and all its monuments, softly fringed with trees, and set in a heavenly firmament. And the Pilgrim thought of those words that described this lovely place as a bride adorned for her husband, and did not wonder at him who had said that her streets were of gold and her gates of pearl, because gold and pearls and precious jewels were as nothing to the glory and the beauty of her. The little Pilgrim was glad to have seen these wonderful things, and her mind was like a cup running over with almost more than it could contain. It seemed to her that there never could be a time when she should want for wonder and interest and delight so long as she had this to think of. Yet she was not sorry to turn her back upon the beautiful city, but went on her way singing in unutterable content, and thinking over what the lady had said, that we were in God's secret, more than all the great worlds above and even the angels, because of knowing how it is that in darkness and doubt, and without any open vision, a man may still keep the right way. The path lay along the bank of the river which flowed beside her and made the air full of music, and a soft air blew across the running stream and breathed in her face and refreshed her, and the birds sang in all the trees. And as she passed through the villages the people came out to meet her, and asked of her if she had come from the city, and what she had seen there. And everywhere she found friends, and kind voices that gave her greeting. But some would ask her why she still spoke the little language, though it was sweet to their ears; and others when they heard it hastened to call from the houses and the fields some among them who knew the other tongue but a little, and who came and crowded round the little Pilgrim and asked her many questions both about the things she had been seeing and about the old time. And she perceived that the village folk were a simple folk, not learned and wise like those she had left. And that though they lived within sight of the great city, and showed every stranger the beautiful view of it, and the glory of its towers, yet few among them had travelled there; for they were so content with their fields and their river, and the shade of their trees and the birds singing, and their simple life, that they wanted no change; though it pleased them to receive the little Pilgrim, and they brought her in to their villages rejoicing, and called every one to see her. And they told her that they had all been poor and laboured hard in the old time, and had never rested; so that now it was the Father's good pleasure that they should enjoy great peace and consolation among the fresh-breathing fields and on the riverside, so that there were many who even now had little occupation except to think of the Father's goodness and to rest. And they told her how the Lord Himself would come among them, and sit down under a tree, and tell them one of His parables, and make them all more happy than words could say; and how sometimes He would send one out of the beautiful city, with a poem or tale to say to them, and bands of lovely music, more lovely than anything beside, except the sound of the Lord's own voice. "And what is more wonderful, the angels themselves come often and listen to us," they said, "when we begin to talk and remind each other of the old time, and how we suffered heat and cold, and were bowed down with labour, and bending over the soil; and how sometimes the harvest would fail us, and sometimes we had not bread, and sometimes would hush the children to sleep because there was nothing to give them; and how we grew old and weary, and still worked on and on." "We are those who were old," a number of them called out to her, with a murmuring sound of laughter, one looking over another's shoulder. And one woman said, "The angels say to us, 'Did you never think the

Father had forsaken you and the Lord forgotten you?'"
And all the rest answered as in a chorus, "There were
moments that we thought this; but all the time we knew
that it could not be." "And the angels wonder at us," said
another. All this they said, crowding one before another,
every one anxious to say something, and sometimes
speaking together, but always in accord. And then there
was a sound of laughter and pleasure, both at the strange
thought that the Lord could have forgotten them, and at
the wonder of the angels over their simple tales. And
immediately they began to remind each other, and say,
"Do you remember?" and they told the little Pilgrim a
hundred tales of the hardships and troubles they had
known, all smiling and radiant with pleasure; and at every
new account the others would applaud and rejoice,
feeling the happiness all the more for the evils that were
past. And some of them led her into their gardens to show
her their flowers, and to tell her how they had begun to
study and learn how colours were changed and form per-
fected, and the secrets of the growth and of the germ of
which they had been ignorant. And others arranged
themselves in choirs, and sang to her delightful songs of
the fields, and accompanied her out upon her way,
singing and answering to each other. The difference
between the simple folk and the greatness of the others
made the little Pilgrim wonder and admire, and she loved
them in her simplicity, and turned back many a time to
wave her hand to them, and to listen to the lovely simple
singing as it went farther and farther away. It had an evening tone of rest and quietness, and of protection and
peace. "He leadeth me by the green pastures and beside
the quiet waters," she said to herself: and her heart
swelled with pleasure to think that it was those who had
been so old, and so weary and poor, who had this rest to
console them for all their sorrows.

And as she went along, not only did she pass through

many other villages, but met many on the way who were travelling towards the great city, and would greet her sweetly as they passed, and sometimes stop to say a pleasant word, so that the little Pilgrim was never lonely wherever she went. But most of them began to speak to her in the other language, which was as beautiful and sweet as music, but which she could not understand: and they were surprised to find her ignorant of it, not knowing that she was but a new-comer into these lands. And there were many things that could not be told but in that language, for the earthly tongue had no words to express them. The little Pilgrim was a little sad not to understand what was said to her, but cheered herself with the thought that it should be taught to her by one whom she loved best. The way by the riverside was very cheerful and bright, with many people coming and going, and many villages, some of them with a bridge across the stream, some withdrawn among the fields, but all of them bright and full of life, and with sounds of music, and voices, and footsteps: and the little Pilgrim felt no weariness, but moved along as lightly as a child, taking great pleasure in everything she saw, and answering all the friendly greetings with all her heart, yet glad to think that she was approaching ever nearer to the country where it was ordained that she should dwell for a time and succour the strangers, and receive those who were newly arrived. And she consoled herself with the thought that there was no need of any language but that which she knew. As this went through her mind making her glad she suddenly became aware of one who was walking by her side, a lady who was covered with a veil white and shining like that which Ama had worn in the beautiful city. It hung about this stranger's head so that it was not easy to see her face, and the sound of her voice was very sweet in the Pilgrim's ear, yet startled her like the sound of something which she knew well, but could not remember. And as there were few who were going that way, she was glad, and said, "Let us walk together, if that pleases you." And the stranger said, "It is for that I have come," which was a reply which made the little Pilgrim wonder more and more, though she was very glad and joyful to have this companion upon her way. And then the lady began to ask her many questions, not about the city, or the great things she had seen, but about herself, and what the dear Lord had given her to do.

"I am little and weak, and I cannot do much," the little Pilgrim said. "It is nothing but pleasure. It is to welcome those that are coming, and tell them. Sometimes they are astonished and do not know. I was so myself. I came in my sleep, and understood nothing. But now that I know, it is sweet to tell them that they need not fear."

"I was glad," the lady said, "that you came in your sleep: for sometimes the way is dark and hard, and you are little and tender. When your brother comes you will be the first to see him, and show him the way."

"My brother! is he coming?" the little Pilgrim cried. And then she said with a wistful look, "But we are all brethren, and you mean only one of those who are the children of our Father. You must forgive me that I do not know the higher speech, but only what is natural, for I have not yet been long here."

"He whom I mean is called—" and here the lady said a name which was the true name of a brother born, whom the Pilgrim loved above all others. She gave a cry, and then she said trembling, "I know your voice, but I cannot see your face. And what you say makes me think of many things. No one else has covered her face when she has spoken to me. I know you, and yet I cannot tell who you are."

The woman stood for a little without saying a word, and then very softly, in a voice which only the heart heard, she called the little Pilgrim by her name.

"*Mother*," cried the Pilgrim, with such a cry of joy that it echoed all about in the sweet air: and flung herself upon the veiled lady, and drew the veil from her face, and saw that it was she. And with this sight there came a revelation which flooded her soul with happiness. For the face which had been old and feeble was old no longer, but fair in the maturity of day; and the figure that had been bent and weary was full of a tender majesty, and the arms that clasped her about were warm and soft with love and life. And all that had changed their relations in the other days and made the mother in her weakness seem as a child, and transferred all protection and strength to the daughter, was gone for ever: and the little Pilgrim beheld in a rapture one who was her sister and equal, yet ever above her—more near to her than any, though all were so near—one of whom she herself was a part, yet another, and who knew all her thoughts and the way of them before they arose in her. And to see her face as in the days of her prime, and her eyes so clear and wise, and to feel once more that which is different from the love of all, that which is still most sweet where all is sweet, the love of one—was like a crown to her in her happiness. The little Pilgrim could not think for joy, nor say a word, but held this dear mother's hands and looked in her face, and her heart soared away to the Father in thanks and joy. They sat down by the roadside under the shade of the trees, while the river ran softly by, and everything was hushed out of sympathy and kindness, and questioned each other of all that had been and was to be. And the little Pilgrim told all the little news of home, and of the brothers and sisters and the children that had been born, and of those whose faces were turned towards this better country; and the mother smiled and listened and would have heard all over and over, although many things she already knew. "But why should I tell you? for did not you watch over us and see all we did, and were not you near us always?" the little Pilgrim said.

"How could that be?" said the mother; "for we are not like our Lord, to be everywhere. We come and go where we are sent. But sometimes we knew and sometimes saw, and always loved. And whenever our hearts were sick for news it was but to go to Him, and He told us everything. And now, my little one, you are as we are, and have seen the Lord. And this has been given us, to teach our child once more, and show you the heavenly language, that you may understand all, both the little and the great."

Then the Pilgrim lifted her head from her mother's bosom, and looked in her face with eyes full of longing. "You said 'we,'" she said.

The mother did nothing but smile; then lifted her eyes and looked along the beautiful path of the river to where some one was coming to join them; and the little Pilgrim cried out again, in wonder and joy; and presently found herself seated between them, her father and her mother, the two who had loved her most in the other days. They looked more beautiful than the angels and all the great persons whom she had seen; for still they were hers and she was theirs, more than all the angels and all the blessed could be. And thus she learned that though the new may take the place of the old, and many things may blossom out of it like flowers, yet that the old is never done away. And then they sat together, telling of everything that had befallen, and all the little tender things that were of no import, and all the great changes and noble ways, and the wonders of heaven above and the earth beneath, for all were open to them, both great and small; and when they had satisfied their souls with these, her father and mother began to teach her the other language, smiling often at her faltering tongue, and telling her the same thing over and over till she learned it; and her father called her his little foolish one, as he had done in the old days; and at last, when they had kissed her and blessed her, and told her how to come home to them when she was weary, they gave her, as the Father had permitted them, with joy and blessing, her new name.

The little Pilgrim was tired with happiness and all the wonder and pleasure, and as she sat there in the silence leaning upon those who were so dear to her, the soft air grew sweeter and sweeter about her, and the light faded softly into a dimness of tender indulgence and privilege for her, because she was still little and weak. And whether that heavenly suspense of all her faculties was sleep or not she knew not, but it was such as in all her life she had never known. When she came back to herself, it was by the sound of many voices calling her, and many people hastening past and beckoning to her to join them.

"Come, come," they said, "little sister: there has been great trouble in the other life, and many have arrived suddenly and are afraid. Come, come, and help them—come and help them!"

And she sprang up from her soft seat, and found that she was no longer by the riverside, or within sight of the great city or in the arms of those she loved, but stood on one of the flowery paths of her own border-land, and saw her fellows hastening towards the gates where there seemed a great crowd. And she was no longer weary, but full of life and strength, and it seemed to her that she could take them up in her arms, those trembling strangers, and carry them straight to the Father, so strong was she, and light, and full of force. And above all the gladness she had felt, and all her pleasure in what she had seen, and more happy even than the meeting with those she loved most, was her happiness now, as she went along as light as the breeze to receive the strangers. She was so eager that she began to sing a song of welcome as she hastened on. "Oh, welcome, welcome!" she cried; and as she sang she knew it was one of the heavenly melodies which she had heard in the great city: and she hastened on, her feet flying over the flowery ways, thinking how the great worlds were all watching, and the angels looking on, and the whole universe waiting till it should be proved to them that the dear Lord, the Brother of us all, had chosen the perfect way, and that over all the evil and the sorrow He was the Conqueror alone.

And the little Pilgrim's voice, though it was so small, echoed away through the great firmament to where the other worlds were watching to see what should come, and cheered the anxious faces of some great lords and princes far more great than she, who were of a nobler race than man; for it was said among the stars that when such a little sound could reach so far, it was a token that the Lord had chosen aright, and that His method must be the best. And it breathed over the earth like some one saying, Courage! to those whose hearts were failing; and it dropped down, down, into the great confusions and traffic of the Land of Darkness, and startled many, like the cry of a child calling and calling, and never ceasing, "Come! and come! and come!"

THE END.